In Search
of the
Perfect Pumpkin

Gloria Evangelista
Illustrated by Shawn Shea

FULCRUM

GOLDEN, COLORADO

I was as high as a baseball bat, skinny as one too, when Mom decided to bake fresh pumpkin pies for fall, and so we went in search of the perfect pumpkin.

What are the world's largest fruits? Pumpkins. The largest ones can weigh more than 1,000 pounds!

We purchased our pumpkins at the local grocery store the first year.

A sign read, "**SUGAR PUMPKINS! GREAT FOR BAKING!**"

I asked the produce man, "How great are these pumpkins? Are they 'Hooray, the Red Sox won again!' kind of great, or are they 'Due to the weather, all schools will be closed until further notice' kind of great?"

I definitely preferred the second.

He said, "Don't know. Never baked with sugar pumpkins before."

How to pick a perfect pumpkin: make sure it's firm all over, but especially firm on the bottom.

We took our chances and bought the pumpkins because we're chance-taking kind of people, the kind who ride in the front seat of the Killer Cyclops or meander through the woods with slithering rattlesnakes and screeching coyotes.

Pumpkins were once recommended for removing freckles and curing snakebites.

The sugar pumpkins made good pies, not Red Sox winning, school closing kind of pies, but everyone liked them. Even our dog Bonkers seemed pleased when my sister shared a piece with him, although Mom wasn't too happy.

Pumpkin pie was not eaten at the Thanksgiving feast, nor for that matter was anything sweet. What supply of sugar the Pilgrims brought on the *Mayflower* had dwindled by the time of the feast. Also, Pilgrims did not have ovens.

The next year we drove to a pumpkin patch in search of the perfect pumpkin. A scarecrow right out of *The Wizard of Oz* pointed to an entire mound of them with a sign that read, **"UNBELIEVABLE PIE PUMPKINS."**

In early colonial America, pumpkins were used as an ingredient for the crust of pies, not the filling.

I asked, "How unbelievable are these pumpkins? Are they 'Our turtle lived in the vacuum cleaner for an entire month and is still alive' unbelievable, or are they 'You just won $500 worth of merchandise from the toy store, shop-till-you-drop' unbelievable?"

"These pumpkins are truly unbelievable," the lady said. "They were grown in the rich valleys of Iowa, picked fresh, and hauled here."

The only thing I found unbelievable was the fact that Iowa is far away and her truck looked as if it couldn't make it around the corner. I snooped around for a Batmobile. However, we felt if the pumpkins were good enough for Dorothy and Toto, they were good enough for us.

The pumpkins from Iowa made good pies, not your turtle lived in a vacuum cleaner, go raid the toy store kind of pies, but everyone liked them.

Even my sister refused to share, although I'm not sure if it was because she liked the pie so much or was just tired of scrubbing it off the floor.

Pumpkins have been food sources, symbols, and even toys for longer than recorded history.

The next year we went organic. I was just glad we weren't going to Iowa. We drove to a farm where all the fruits and vegetables are grown without the use of chemical sprays or pesticides. Those are things that farmers use to keep pests like bugs and rabbits away.

I wondered if they worked on sisters.

"You want Sugar Babies," the man said. "They're scrumptious for baking."

"How scrumptious are they?" I asked. "Are they 'gooey cheese pizza right out of the oven' kind of scrumptious? Or are they 'melt in your mouth, drippy chocolate and marshmallow s'mores, gotta have another' kind of scrumptious?"

Either one of those would be fine with me.

One pumpkin plant normally produces 3 to 5 pumpkins, sometimes more. Miniature varieties produce about 1 dozen.

He said, "They're 'You'd better buy them now because I'm not picking any more until Thanksgiving' kind of scrumptious."

We knew a good thing when we saw it.

Pumpkins have been grown in America for more than 5,000 years and were completely unknown in Europe before the time of Columbus.

The organic Sugar Babies pumpkins made good pies, not gooey cheese pizza right out of the oven pies or melt in your mouth gotta have another kind of pies, but everyone liked them.

The Native Americans of the eastern United States considered pumpkin almost as important a food as corn and beans. They baked and boiled pumpkins, and ground the seeds into meal for gruel and bread.

Thus, another year passed and we remained in search of the perfect pumpkin.

Finally, Mom announced, "This year we will grow our own pumpkins."

Dad said they will be the greatest, most unbelievably scrumptious pumpkins of all, and Dad knows everything, like if you walk barefoot on the moon you'll get sticky marshmallow feet and to never attempt to climb Mount Everest if you eat only cookies for breakfast.

The single most important factor in determining where to locate a pumpkin patch is to make sure it gets lots of sun.

And so our garden began.
We planted,
we watered,
we weeded,
we hoed.
Took but a week for those
seeds to explode.
We covered,
we fertilized,
we prayed for
no snow.

Tips: Soak seeds in warm water for 1 or 2 hours before planting. Plant the seeds 1-inch deep, pointed end down. That's where the root will come out.

Leaves sprawled in the yard, they sprawled in the road.

Soon a green vine grew to a bright yellow flower, and a bulb followed that, then a ball then I hollered…

The flowers of pumpkins are edible.

Do chirping birds and crickets help plants grow? Yes! Scientists have found that certain sounds cause pores in plant leaves to open, resulting in stronger growth.

There were pumpkins here, there were pumpkins there, there were pumpkins **_EVERYWHERE_**!

In China, the pumpkin is the emperor of the garden—symbol of fruitfulness, health, and reward.

We named them
Portabello,
Monticello,
Sneakers, and Sublime,
Mammaletti,
Somba-getti,
Tweekers, and
Past Prime.
There was Dollarwise
and Penny Foolish,
News at Five and
Hammer Tool-Dish.

One pumpkin plant, which was grown from a seed won in a raffle, produced 2,715 pounds of pumpkin. The plant's 4 pumpkins weighed 774, 686, 652, and 603 pounds. All were healthy.

Hackety Sackety and
    Pumpernickel
        smelled like a melon,
            looked like a pickle.
Quasimodo and
    Toto, too,
        sprawled around
            this pumpkin zoo.

What do the names Munchkin,
Baby Boo, Jackpot, Frosty, Ghost
Rider, Jumpin' Jack, Big Max,
and Gremlin describe? All are
different varieties of pumpkins.

We picked them,
we washed them,
we seeded, and
we baked.
We made pies,
we made breads,
we made
orange fruitcake.
And do you know what?

A 4-pound pumpkin yields about
4 cups of mashed pumpkin meat;
2 cups make 1 pie.

Our pumpkins made the greatest, most unbelievably scrumptious, Red Sox-winning, school-closing, turtle-alive-in-a-vacuum-cleaner, gooey-cheese-pizza-right-out-of-the-oven, melt-in-your-mouth-s'mores kind of pies anyone ever tasted.

Make horns from the hollow stems of pumpkins: Cut off the stalk, scrape off the prickles, then put the hollow end in your mouth and blow. Big stalks make a mooing sound.

From The Kitchen Of...

The Perfect Pumpkin Pie

2 cups fresh pumpkin (slightly chunky)
2/3 cup sugar
1/2 tsp. salt
3 1/4 tsp. pumpkin pie spice
3 slightly beaten eggs
5/8 cup nonfat milk (use whole milk, if preferred)
6 oz. evaporated milk
9-in. unbaked pastry shell, preferably deep dish

For a deep-dish pie you will need approximately one pumpkin per pie. Cut pumpkin in half and place face down in a baking dish in about an inch of water. Bake at 350 degrees Fahrenheit until soft. Do not overcook. Remove the seeds and peeling. Mash pumpkin in bowl until slightly chunky, not whipped.

Combine pumpkin, sugar, salt, and spices. Blend in eggs, milk, and evaporated milk. Pour mixture into pastry shell (crimp edges high, as amount is generous). Cover edges of crust with foil until a few minutes before pie is done, then remove to brown.

Bake at 400 degrees Fahrenheit for about 45 minutes or until inserted knife comes out clean. Cool. Place pecan halves on top to decorate, if desired. Serve with vanilla ice cream and a dollop of whipped cream. Enjoy.

Dedicated to Michael, Josh, and Zach, as well as Tony, Liz, and Taylor...for Evangelistas, not unlike pumpkins, never fail to multiply.

Text © 2001, 2008 Gloria Evangelista
Illustrations © 2001, 2008 Shawn Shea

Library of Congress Cataloging-in-Publication Data

Evangelista, Gloria.
  In search of the perfect pumpkin / Gloria Evangelista ; illustrated by Shawn Shea.
    p. cm.
  ISBN-13: 978-1-55591-697-8 (pbk.)
  1. Pumpkin--Juvenile literature. 2. Cookery (Pumpkin)--Juvenile literature. I. Shea, Shawn. II. Title.
  SB347.E93 2008
  635'.62--dc22

                    2008010065

Printed in China
0 9 8 7 6 5 4 3 2 1

Fulcrum Publishing
4690 Table Mountain Drive, Suite 100
Golden, Colorado 80403
www.fulcrumbooks.com